# Would a Worm Go on a Walk?

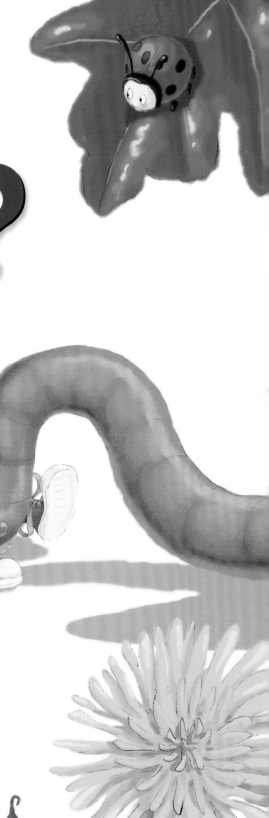

# Would a Worm Go on a Walk?

Written by **Hannah C. Hall**

Illustrated by **Bill Bolton**

Worthy **kids**
**ideals**™

Nashville, Tennessee

ISBN-13: 978-0-8249-5677-6

Published by WorthyKids/Ideals
An imprint of Worthy Publishing Group
A division of Worthy Media, Inc.
Nashville, Tennessee

Text copyright © 2016 by Hannah C. Hall
Art copyright © 2016 by Bill Bolton

Scripture quotation on page 32 is from the *Holy Bible*, New International
Version®, NIV® Copyright ©1973, 1978, 1984, 2011 by Biblica, Inc.®
Used by permission of Zondervan. All rights reserved worldwide.

Library of Congress CIP data on file

Designed by Georgina Chidlow

Printed and bound in China
Wai_Jan16_1

For Gibson, who was the first to ask if a
worm could go on a walk. And for Josh, who
always knew that, one day, it would. —H.H.

For Ben and Amy. —B.B.

Would he wear his tiny tennies
if he had four worm-sized feet?

Would a worm go on a walk?

NO! No matter how he tries,
worms weren't made for walking,
and they don't like EXERCISE.

Would a piglet play piano?

NO! 'Cause music's not her thing.
Hooves weren't made for Mozart,
and she'd rather SQUEAL than sing.

Would a LADYBUG wear lipstick?

NO! That's not what she enjoys.
'Cause lipstick is for ladies,
and some ladybugs are BOYS.

Would a rhino wear a raincoat?

NO! Rain doesn't bother him.
Rhinos don't need rain gear.
Their slickers are built-in.

Would a lion be a lifeguard?

NO! No way he ever would.
Lions don't like water.
That is CLEARLY understood.

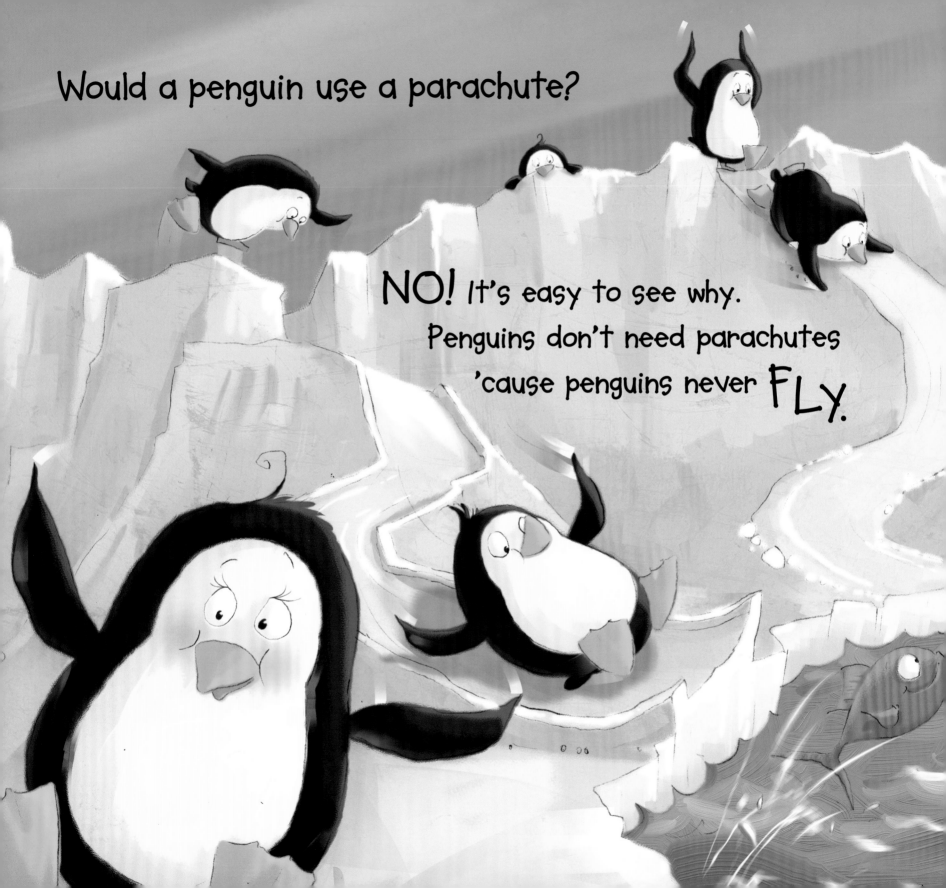

Would a penguin use a parachute?

NO! It's easy to see why.
Penguins don't need parachutes
'cause penguins never FLY.

Would a POSSUM like to polka
if you could teach him how to dance?

Would he prefer to TANGO
if he learned the proper stance?

Would a possum like to polka?

**DANCE HALL**

**NO!** He'd be just sick with dread.
Possums get too nervous,
so they end up PLAYING DEAD.

Would a TURTLE drive a truck
if she had to get to town?

Or would she like a SKATEBOARD as a way to get around?

Would a turtle drive a truck?

NO!
A truck goes
WAY TOO
FAST.

Turtles like to take it slow.
They tend to come in last.

So turtles wouldn't drive,

and possums wouldn't dance.

Lion's manes look lousy wet,

and flying penguins?

Not a chance.

Bugs don't like to froo-froo,

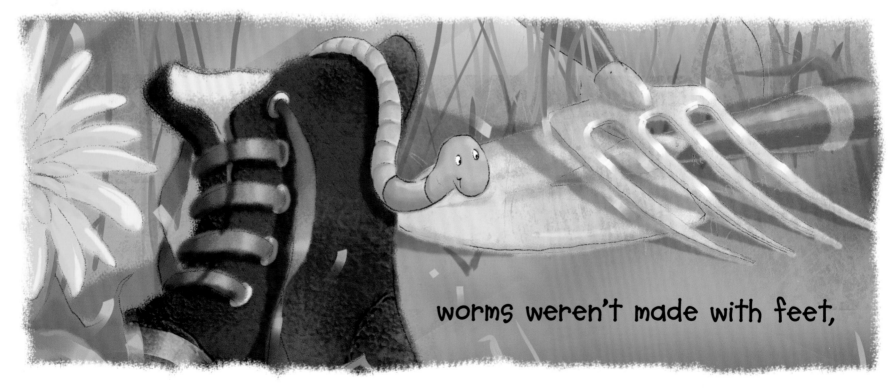

worms weren't made with feet,

the rhino's rain-resistant,

and the pig can't keep a beat.

But each was formed on purpose,
by a wise Creator God.

He planned their every detail,
both the normal and the odd.

They look just as he wanted,
and they act just as they should.
He made them and he loves them,
and he calls them very good.

But God's designs weren't finished.

His special plans weren't through.

The ANIMALS were just a start.
God's masterpiece is YOU!

God saw all that he had
made, and it was very good.
—Genesis 1:31a